First published in the United States, Great Britain, Canada, Australia, and New Zealand in 2008
by North-South Books Inc., an imprint of NordSüd Verlag AG, Zürich, Switzerland.
Distributed in the United States by North-South Books Inc., New York.

Library of Congress Cataloging-in-Publication Data is available.
ISBN: 978-0-7358-2205-4 (trade edition).
2 4 6 8 10 ☀ 9 7 5 3 1
Printed in Belgium

www.northsouth.com

Becky the Borrower

Udo Weigelt

illustrated by Astrid Henn

NorthSouth
New York / London

Becky loved kindergarten. She loved her teacher. She loved all her new friends. She loved show-and-tell. She loved all the toys . . .

From Ricky,
a pair of
roller skates.

From
Barry,
a ball.

From
Andrew, an
airplane.

From Monica,
a monster.

From Benjy,
some
balloons.

From
Willie,
a water
pistol.

From Patty,
some
playing cards.

. . . *and* she loved to borrow things.

From Betsy, some blocks.

From Pearla, some beautiful glass pearls.

From Bettina, a bug bottle.

From Timmy, a stuffed tiger.

From Penny, a paint box.

From Claudia, a clown.

From Regina, a race car.

From Dory, a doll.

Becky really did borrow a lot.
It was such fun trying out everything.

"Tell me, Becky," said Daddy, scratching his head. "Why are you always borrowing things? You have plenty of toys of your own, haven't you?"

"I do," said Becky. "But I like these things too. And I just play with them for a little while. I give them back right away."

"Really?" said Daddy. "You give them back right away?"

"Well . . ." Becky looked around. Then she scratched her head too.

At bedtime, Becky looked around her room again. She guessed she had borrowed a lot of things she hadn't given back yet. She wondered who some of them really belonged to.

That night, Becky had a terrible dream. All of the children she had borrowed things from were standing in front of her door. Ten kids. Twenty kids. Too many kids to count.

Then Penny came to the door. "You borrowed something from me," she said. "I want it back now." But she wouldn't tell Becky what it was. Becky kept bringing things out, but nothing was the right thing.

It was the same with the other children. They all wanted their things back, but no one would tell her *which* things. Becky was feeling desperate. She just could not remember what she had borrowed from which child.

"Becky, wake up!" said Mommy.

Whew! thought Becky. It was only a dream. There she was, back in her room with all her toys—and all of everyone else's toys. Who *did* they all belong to? She really *couldn't* remember.

There was only one thing to do. She would take *everything* to kindergarten tomorrow.

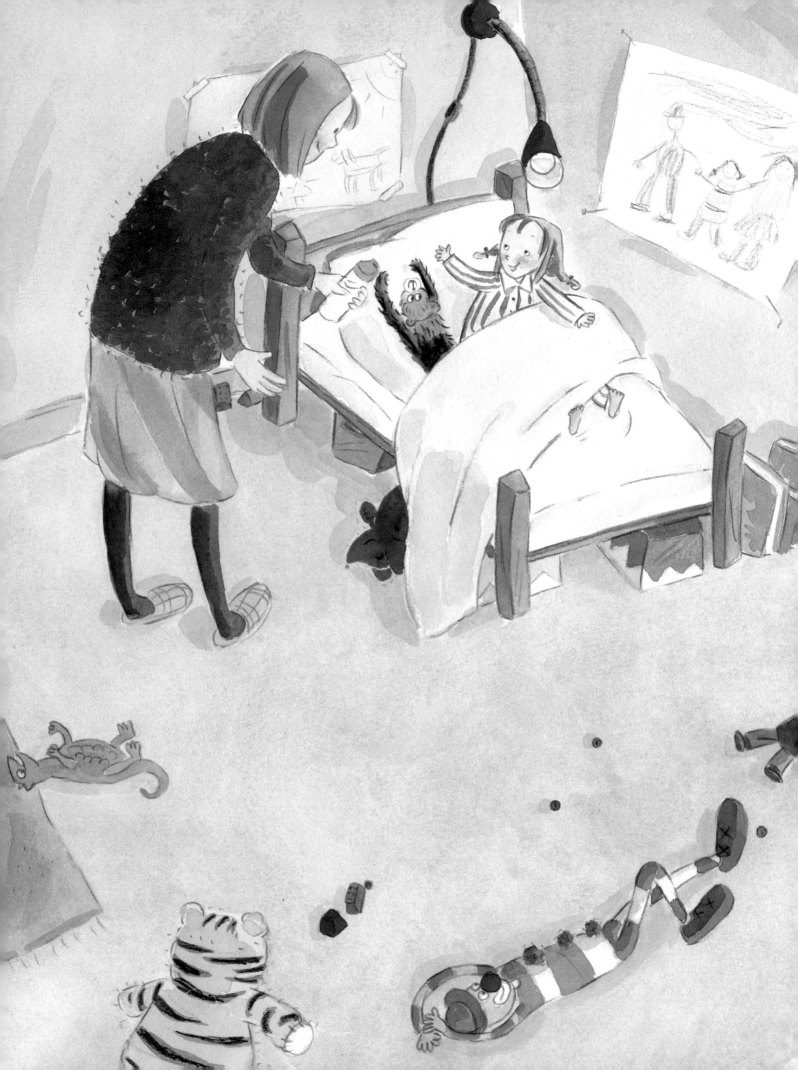

It took three bags to pack up everything, and some things she wasn't so sure about. Did she borrow that tiger, or was it a present from Uncle Otto? And what about that paint box? Wasn't that from Aunt Tanya?

Mommy was surprised. "Becky!" she cried. "You picked up your room all by yourself! That's a first!"
Daddy was speechless.
There was just one thing left to do.

"Will you make me a sign, Daddy?" Becky asked.
"Sure thing," said Daddy. "What will it say?"
"Special today. Return of borrowed things. Everything
free. And Thank you!" Becky told him.

The next day, Becky turned a desk into a store counter and propped up her sign. Soon the children were lining up. Penny was first.

"What will it be today?" Becky asked her.

"I'd like my paint box back," said Penny.

"Certainly, ma'am," said Becky. "Returned with thanks."

Soon all of the children got their things back. Just one thing remained—a shaggy bear. "This must be my very own," said Becky.

"Can I borrow that?" asked Penny.